USBORNE
ILLUSTRATED
FAIRY
TALES

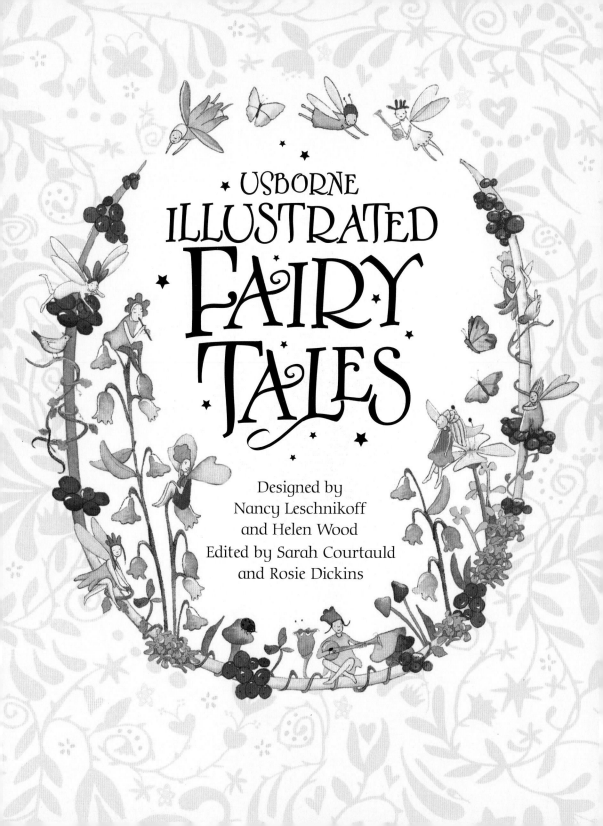

USBORNE
ILLUSTRATED
FAIRY TALES

Designed by
Nancy Leschnikoff
and Helen Wood
Edited by Sarah Courtauld
and Rosie Dickins

Contents

Sleeping Beauty   6

Based on a story by the Brothers Grimm,
retold by Kate Knighton, illustrated by Jana Costa

The Emperor and the Nightingale   44

Based on a story by Hans Christian Andersen,
retold by Rosie Dickins, illustrated by Graham Philpot

Beauty and the Beast   78

Based on a story by Gabrielle de Villeneuve,
retold by Louie Stowell, illustrated by Victor Tavares

The Dragon Painter   120

Based on a Chinese Folk Tale,
retold by Rosie Dickins, illustrated by John Nez

The Frog Prince   150

Based on a story by Hans Christian Andersen,
retold by Susanna Davidson, illustrated by Mike Gordon

The Elves and the Shoemaker   184

Based on a story by the Brothers Grimm,
retold by Katie Daynes, illustrated by Desideria Guicciardini

Little Red Riding Hood   210

Based on a story by the Brothers Grimm,
retold by Susanna Davidson, illustrated by Mike Gordon

Cinderella   242

Based on a story by Charles Perrault,
retold by Susanna Davidson, illustrated by Fabiano Florin

The Swan Princess   276

Based on a story by Hans Christian Andersen,
retold by Rosie Dickins, illustrated by Jenny Press

The Emperor's New Clothes   316

Based on a story by Hans Christian Andersen,
retold by Susanna Davidson, illustrated by Mike Gordon

Sleeping Beauty

Long ago, a king and queen
lived in a magical castle...

...where they had everything they could possibly want – except a baby.

Year after year, the Queen stitched and sewed tiny clothes. And the King spent long afternoons in his palace workshop, making beautiful toys.

But still there was no baby.

Sleeping Beauty

One day, while the Queen sat
knitting by the lake, a bright
green frog hopped, skipped, and
jumped, right onto her lap.

"You shall have a
baby, Your Majesty,"
said the frog.

And with that, he
bowed and leaped
back into the lake.

True to the frog's words, the Queen gave birth to a beautiful baby girl.

"Let's call her Rose," the Queen said happily. The King was so pleased, he planned a great feast to celebrate.

He asked seven fairies to be
Rose's fairy godmothers.

On the night of the
feast, they all flew into
the castle, each
clasping a glittering
golden wand.

"Let the feast begin!" announced the Queen, and merry music filled the Great Hall.

The tables were piled high with scrumptious food, and everyone ate off silver plates.

When no one could manage
another bite, the fairies gathered
before the King and Queen.

"We have some wishes for Princess Rose,"
said Snowdrop, the first fairy, with a curtsy.

She fluttered her fairy fingers.

Rose will be utterly beautiful.

Then Honeysuckle waved her wand.

She'll be as clever as the King!

The third fairy, Willow, floated over
to the child.

She will be graceful...

and she'll dance to perfection!

added Bluebell.

Blossom and Buttercup wished that
Rose would...

play music like an angel...

and...

sing like a nightingale.

Everyone wondered what Jasmine, the
seventh and wisest fairy, would wish for.

As Jasmine hovered over the cradle, a blast of icy air swept into the room.

"Haven't you forgotten someone?" a chilling voice rang out.

Suddenly, the mean fairy Nightshade
appeared in a whirlwind of foul
green smoke.

"How DARE you not invite me?" she roared.

"W-we didn't mean to, Nightshade," the King stammered. "We just... f-forgot you."

"FORGOT ME?" Nightshade screamed, so fiercely the flames in the fireplace went out.

"Well, you won't forget this!" She
flicked her cloak and marched up to the
cradle. "Now, my pretty," she purred,
lifting a golden curl with a bony finger,
"what shall I wish for you?"

Everyone in the palace held their breath.
Nightshade leaned down into the cradle.

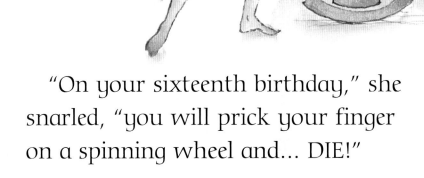

"On your sixteenth birthday," she
snarled, "you will prick your finger
on a spinning wheel and... DIE!"

"No!" cried the Queen. But Nightshade
cackled gleefully and disappeared with a bang.
"I still have my wish," said Jasmine softly.
"I can't undo that wicked spell, but I
can try to change it."

"You will prick your finger, little Rose," Jasmine began, "but you won't die. You and everyone else in the castle will fall into a deep sleep."

Only a kiss from your true love will break the spell.

"Burn every spinning wheel in the land at once!" roared the King. "Rose must never, ever see one!"

That night, the flames from the enormous bonfire could be seen for miles. They licked the dark sky like serpents' tongues.

The years passed
and Rose turned
into a delightful girl.
She danced, sang
and played music as
wonderfully as the
fairies had wished.

She was clever enough to beat
the King at chess.

Ha!
Checkmate!

She loved playing hide-and-seek in
the castle gardens.

And, secretly, she liked to sketch the
prince of her dreams.

On her sixteenth birthday, the King
and Queen gave a huge ball for Rose.

She swirled and twirled in a dazzling ball
gown and every prince fell in love with her.

When the feasting was nearly
over, Rose pleaded for a game.
"Hide-and-seek!" she shouted
and dashed off into the castle.
She raced up a twisting
staircase that she had
never seen before.

Soft singing floated down the stairs.
In a trance, Rose followed the music.

At the top of the stairs, she discovered
a heavy iron door.

Inside, an old woman sat
hunched over a spinning wheel.
  "Come and see, my pretty,"
she said, beckoning Rose
with a bony finger.

"I'm spinning, my dear," croaked the old woman.

"May I try?" asked Rose, touching the silky thread.

"Of course," said the old woman, taking her hand.

At once, Rose snapped out
of the trance. "Ow!" she cried,
as she pricked her finger.

Rose fell to the floor. The old woman
cackled and disappeared in a whirlwind
of foul green smoke.

In the same instant, everyone in the castle fell asleep.

The King dozed off with a spoon in his hand...

and the court jester froze mid-leap.

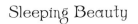

All the clocks stopped. The place was silent and still... except for the rose bushes. They spread like ivy, covering everything in their path.

They grew so quickly that soon the entire castle was covered in thick roots and sharp thorns.

For one hundred years the castle
stayed hidden. Only the tops of the towers
showed through the bushes.

Princes from far and wide heard about the spell. They came in their hundreds to try to rescue the princess known as Sleeping Beauty.

But the thorns cut their skin and the roots wrapped around their legs like snakes, until they all gave up.

One day, a brave prince named
Florien rode by. He had dreamed
of Sleeping Beauty and was
determined to find her.

He pulled out his sword with a flourish
and began to fight his way through the
spiky bushes.

As Florien's sword touched a
branch, each sharp thorn became
a sweet-smelling rose.

A path cleared before him. He followed
its twists and turns until he reached the
topmost turret where Sleeping Beauty lay.

Florien's heart fluttered like a bird when he saw her. She was the most beautiful girl he had ever seen.

Taking her hand, he kissed her soft lips. Her eyes flickered open and Rose found herself face to face with the prince of her dreams.

"You're the prince I drew!" she cried.
"Prince Florien here to rescue you,"
he announced and scooped her up.

As they walked through tunnels of roses,
everyone else in the castle began to wake up.

The King fell into his pudding with
an enormous splosh...

and the court jester landed with an
unexpected bump.

Ow!

Rose and Florien entered the Great Hall.
"My Rose!" cried the Queen.
"And her true love," added the King.

Rose and Florien were married the next day. They lived happily ever after – and the Prince always lost at chess.

The Emperor and the Nightingale

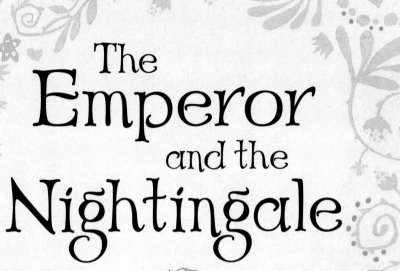

The Emperor of China lived
in a palace full of treasures...

...which came from all over the world. He had beautiful paintings and glittering jewels, and even his dog wore a fine silk coat.

The palace garden was so big that even the Emperor never saw it all. He never saw the little nightingale who lived in the trees.

But the gardener saw her every day. He liked to listen to her singing.

Her songs always made
him smile.

One day, the Emperor was reading a book about his wonderful palace.

The book said: "The Emperor's garden is full of bells that tinkle sweetly." The Emperor smiled proudly.

But the book went on: "The nightingale's song sounds sweeter than the bells!"

"Why haven't I heard this nightingale?" snapped the Emperor.

Bring it to sing in the palace— NOW!

The palace servants didn't know anything about the nightingale. But they didn't dare tell the Emperor.

They searched high and low...

What's a nightingale?

Where can we find it?

In the end, they had to ask the gardener. "Follow me," he said, smiling. "I can show you the nightingale." He led the servants through the garden.

They walked and walked, until suddenly, they heard a croak.

"The nightingale!" cried the servants.

What sweet singing!

ribbit-ribbit!

The gardener smiled. "No, that's a frog in the pond," he replied.

A little later, they heard a loud moo.
"The nightingale!" cried the servants.

What a voice!

"No, that's a cow in the field," the gardener told them. He was trying not to laugh.

In the end, they came to the tree, and heard the real nightingale singing.

"Little bird," said the servants, "the Emperor wants you to sing in his palace."

Che-che-cheer up!

Che-che-cheer up!

Such sweet music.

Ssshh!

"My songs sound best out here, among
the trees," said the bird, "but I will come."
And she flew with them to the palace.

The Emperor was enchanted by the nightingale. He ordered her to stay and sing to him every day. But she missed living outside, among the trees.

Soon, the little brown bird was famous.
Even the Emperor of Japan
came to hear her sing.

Che-che-cheer up!

One day, a package arrived at the palace. Inside there was another nightingale. This one had sparkling golden feathers and ruby eyes.

To the Emperor of China, from the Emperor of Japan

Here's an even better nightingale!

Chee~cluck!

When you turned a key, it sang like the little brown bird – well, sort of...

The Emperor was very happy.
He was so happy that he forgot all about
the little brown bird. She flew away – and
nobody noticed.

The Emperor played the golden nightingale every morning and every evening.

Until one day, instead of singing...

it went *whizz-whirr*
and *ker-plunk*.

Something had broken inside. No one knew how to fix it.

Now the Emperor longed for the little brown bird. He ordered his servants to search for her everywhere. But no one could find her – not even the gardener.

Then the Emperor fell sick. He lay in bed, staring sadly at his broken bird. His room was full of silence and shadows.

The doctors tried every medicine,
but nothing would cure him.
They said he was close to death.

Suddenly, birdsong filled the air. The real nightingale had found out the Emperor was sick, and come back to sing for him.

She sang so sweetly that the shadows
seemed to fade. The Emperor smiled
– and he began to get better.

"Please stay," he begged the little bird.
"You can have a golden cage and all the
servants you want!"

"I prefer to live outside among the trees," the nightingale replied.
And she flew away.

The Emperor was very sad. He asked the gardener to plant a tree under his window.

"It will remind me of the real nightingale," he said.

The gardener watered the tree every day.
It grew and grew.

One day, the Emperor heard something flutter past his window. He looked out.

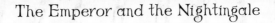

To his surprise, he saw two nightingales. They had built a nest in the tree.

And when they sang, everyone in the palace smiled to hear them – the Emperor most of all.

Beauty
and the
Beast

There was once a very,
very rich man, named Pierre...

...who gave his three daughters *everything* they wanted.

"Bring us emeralds and rubies and silks from the market!" demanded Sophie and Marie, his eldest daughters.

Pierre turned to his youngest daughter, who was standing quietly by.

"Don't you want anything, Beauty?" he asked.

"May I have a rose?" asked Beauty.

Pierre waved goodbye to his daughters
and galloped away on his sleek white horse.
As he rode, a thick fog filled the air.
He went on blindly, until suddenly...

the fog rolled back to reveal a towering castle, looming before him.

"Where am I?" Pierre gasped.
The castle gates opened
slowly before him with a
ghostly creak. Wonderingly,
Pierre rode through the
mist and up to the castle.

The wooden doors were
firmly shut.

As Pierre raised his hand to knock, the
doors swung open by themselves.

"Hello?" he called. No one answered.
He tried again. "Hello?"

But he only heard his own voice,
echoing off the stone walls.

Pierre followed his nose to an enormous feast. He sat down nervously. A full plate floated over to him and he cried out in surprise. But he was cold and starving, and the food smelled so good.

"I hope no one minds," he thought, picking up a silver fork.

Feeling full and tired, Pierre rose from the table. Instantly, a bed appeared before him. Pierre was too exhausted to question it. He just lay down and fell fast asleep.

"I must find the owners and thank them,"
thought Pierre, when he woke. He set out
to search the castle. Invisible hands opened
all the doors, but he couldn't find a single
living person anywhere. "Perhaps everyone's
outside?" he wondered.

In the garden, he found a beautiful
rose bush. As he sniffed the blooms,
he remembered his promise to Beauty.

The instant Pierre plucked a rose, a huge
shadow fell over the rose bushes. He spun
around, clutching the flower to his chest...

A hideous creature stood before him.
"How dare you steal from the Beast?"
roared the creature. "I gave you food and
shelter, and this is how you repay me?
Thief! You'll pay with your life!"

"I'm s-s-sorry," said Pierre. "I just wanted a rose for Beauty – for my daughter."

"A daughter? Hmm... I'll let you live if you send her to me," the Beast declared. "If she refuses, you must return in a week!"

"I can't risk Beauty's life," Pierre thought. With a heavy heart, he told the Beast he would return.

Before Pierre left, the Beast gave him a ruby bridle for his horse. "He'll be able to find his way to your home and back," said the Beast. "The bridle will guide him."

Pierre returned safely home. But
as the week passed, he grew pale.
"What's wrong, Father?"
Beauty wanted to know.
"Nothing," he replied.
"Please don't worry
about me."

That night, Beauty thought
she heard him crying.

She found him asleep at his desk the next morning, with a letter in front of him. She picked it up and started to read.

Dearest daughters,

When you read this letter I will have left you forever. I took a rose from the garden of a monstrous beast and he has sworn to kill me unless I bring him my youngest daughter. I could never do that to you, Beauty, so I have gone in your place.

Farewell,
Your loving Father x x

"Oh no!" cried Beauty. "This is all my fault."

Looking out of the window, Beauty saw her father's horse saddled up, ready to go. She knew what she had to do. Quickly and quietly, she scribbled a note for him, and set off for the castle.

Dear Father,
I have gone to the Beast's
castle instead of you.
All my love,
Beauty

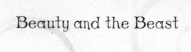

Her father's horse seemed to
know the way. He galloped down
the twisting paths as if guided
by a magic force.

As the Beast's castle came into view,
Beauty gripped the reins in fear. She stopped
at the castle gates, and tiptoed into a sweet
smelling garden. But as soon as she stepped
into the sunlight...

...she heard a terrible growl.

"Who are you?" roared the Beast.

"I'm Beauty, Pierre's daughter," she stammered out.

"He sent you to die, did he?" the Beast growled. "Coward!"

"Don't say that!" said Beauty angrily.

"You have courage," said the Beast,
gazing back at her. As he spoke, Beauty was
shocked to see great tears forming in his eyes.

"What's wrong?" she asked.

"Having you here makes me realize – I've
been alone for so long," he sniffed.

"Poor Beast," said Beauty, her heart filling with pity. "I'll stay with you, if you like."
The Beast grasped her hand, his eyes shining with hope. "Thank you," he said.

But you **must** let my father know I'm safe.

That evening, Beauty and the Beast dined
together. The Beast looked at Beauty very
seriously, then knelt down before her.

"Will you marry me?" he asked.

"I can't," gasped Beauty. "I don't even
know you."

"Very well," said the Beast. He led her to
her room, and wished her goodnight.

Beauty dreamed of home and woke wishing she was there. As she dressed, she saw a mirror by her bed. Peering into it, she was amazed to see her father, back at home.

Seeing him safe and well lifted her spirits. "It's time to explore," she decided.

A magic mirror!

When Beauty went out into the garden, she saw exotic flowers and magical animals.

At eight o'clock, a gong rang for dinner. The Beast was waiting for Beauty in the dining room.

"Did you find the
mirror?" he asked eagerly.
"I loved it. Thank you,"
Beauty replied.

After dinner, the Beast went
down on one knee again.

Beauty sighed. "Beast, you're very
kind, but I don't want to marry you."

"I thought that might be the
answer," said the Beast sadly.

That night, Beauty had a strange
dream. She was dining with a
handsome prince.

"How can you bear to look at that
ugly Beast?" he asked.

"He's not ugly inside," said Beauty.

"But he's a monster," said the Prince.

Beauty awoke to the sound of birds
singing. The Prince had vanished.

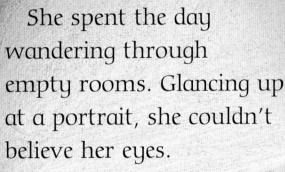

She spent the day wandering through empty rooms. Glancing up at a portrait, she couldn't believe her eyes.

It was the Prince from her dream.

At dinner that evening, she told the Beast about the mysterious prince.

"Do you know who he is?" she asked.

"I know him," replied the Beast. "But I haven't seen him for years."

They sat at the table in silence.

"What's the matter?" the Beast asked eventually, with a worried frown.

"I'm homesick," said Beauty.

The Beast pulled a ring from his pocket.

"Oh Beast, I still won't marry you," she said quickly.

The Beast shook his head. "This isn't a wedding ring. It's magic. It will take you back to your father. But you must promise me you'll return in two weeks."

"I promise," said Beauty happily. "Oh thank you, Beast!"

"Wear the ring on your finger. Then, when you're ready to return, just take it off again."

Beauty nodded. She put on the ring and the room melted away. She felt herself falling... falling... until suddenly she was back at home, and her father was staring at her, open-mouthed.

Beauty's father was overjoyed to see her... unlike her sisters. When they heard her story about the Beast, they hatched a secret plan.

"If we make her stay longer, the Beast will be angry. With any luck, he might even eat her," said Marie, slyly.

"And with Beauty gone, we'll have Father's fortune all to ourselves," added Sophie.

The two weeks flew by, but Beauty kept thinking of the Beast. When the time came for her to leave, her sisters burst out crying.

"We can't live without you!" they howled. "If you loved us, you'd stay!"

Reluctantly, Beauty stayed... until one night, she dreamed she saw the Beast lying in his garden, under a rose bush.

Beauty woke with a start.
"Something's wrong," she
realized. "I must go to him."

Quickly, Beauty took off
the ring. The next instant, a cloud of swirling
smoke surrounded her, and she vanished.

Beauty was back in
the garden. The Beast was
lying under the rose bush,
just as in her dream.
"Is that you Beauty?" he asked.
"I'm dying."

"No!" cried Beauty, horrified. She stroked his velvety face and kissed him. "You can't die! Please, Beast. I love you."

There was a blinding flash.

A handsome prince was kneeling before her.

"You were in my dream... and in the painting!" cried Beauty.

"Many years ago," he explained, "an angry fairy turned me into a Beast because I refused to marry her. Only the love of a beautiful girl could make me human again."

"But why were you dying?" asked Beauty.

"The fairy said if I loved a girl who did not love me, I would die of a broken heart," the Prince replied.

"You don't need to be afraid," said Beauty. "I do love you."

Beauty and the Prince were married the next day, in a church filled with roses.

All of Beauty's family came to the wedding. Her father looked on proudly, but her sisters left early in bad tempers.

"Why does she get to marry a prince?" they complained. "It's not fair!"

"Life isn't fair," said a tiny voice.

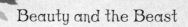

It was the fairy who had set a curse on the Prince. "Your sister broke my spell," she said, "but at least I can give you exactly what you deserve. As you have hearts of stone," the fairy declared, "that's what you'll be... forever!"

Then, feeling much better, she flew off to steal some wedding cake.

The Dragon Painter

High up in the mountains, there
lived a great painter called Chang...

Chang's
House

...everyone loved Chang's beautiful pictures.
They were so lifelike that people came from
all over China to see them.

Splish Splosh

Chang painted misty landscapes and vases
full of flowers. But his animal
pictures were best of all.

:Splash!:

His butterflies and birds really seemed alive. And you could almost see his rabbits twitch their noses.

Chang's pictures soon became famous all over the country. One day, the Emperor of China heard about them.

Now, the Emperor needed someone to decorate his new temple. "I shall ask Chang," he decided.

Chang planned a splendid picture for the temple. On the first wall, he drew a pearl-white dragon. It had long, pointed horns and long, curved claws.

`Splish`

The dragon breathed out huge clouds
of steam. It looked perfect, except for one
thing. The dragon had no eyes.

The second dragon was jade green.
It had a fierce face, with bushy
eyebrows, jagged teeth and a
big, spiky nose.

But the green dragon's eyes were
empty too.

On the third wall, Chang painted a glimmering gold dragon. He gave it a long, coiled tail, curling around its body.

Splish

The gold dragon was nearly complete.
But it didn't have any eyes either.

The fourth and final dragon had a twisting body with gleaming red scales and wicked claws.

Splosh

The red dragon had a terrifying face. But,
just like the others, its eyes were empty.

Chang turned to the Emperor and bowed. "Do you like the dragons, my lord?"

"I do," replied the Emperor. "They're magnificent. There's just one problem – you haven't finished the eyes."

"I can't paint their eyes," said Chang.
"Dragons are magical creatures. If I paint their
eyes, they will come to life."

"Stuff and nonsense!" the Emperor snapped.
"I order you to finish these dragons – at once."

"I can't!" cried Chang. But it was no good. He had to obey the Emperor. With a wobbly hand, he painted the eyes on the first dragon.

sp-sp-splish

There was a rumble of thunder and the
sky grew dark. Chang paused.

"Get on with it!" roared the Emperor.

So he did.

Just as Chang finished...

...a bolt of lightning split open the temple roof.

The jade dragon blinked and looked around. It stretched its arms and slowly raised its head. Its spiky nose cracked one of the temple columns.

Then the pearl dragon opened its eyes and yawned, showing rows of sharp, white teeth. It breathed out burning clouds of steam. The people nearby screamed and ran for their lives.

Suddenly, both dragons jumped from their walls and flew through the hole in the roof.

They flew higher and higher, until
they disappeared into the clouds.

Then the red and gold dragons began to stir. Quickly, Chang grabbed his brush. He painted heavy chains around their necks.

The dragons roared and rattled their chains, but they couldn't fly away.

So, the Emperor had to make do with only two dragons on his temple walls.

But they were the best painted dragons
in all of China.

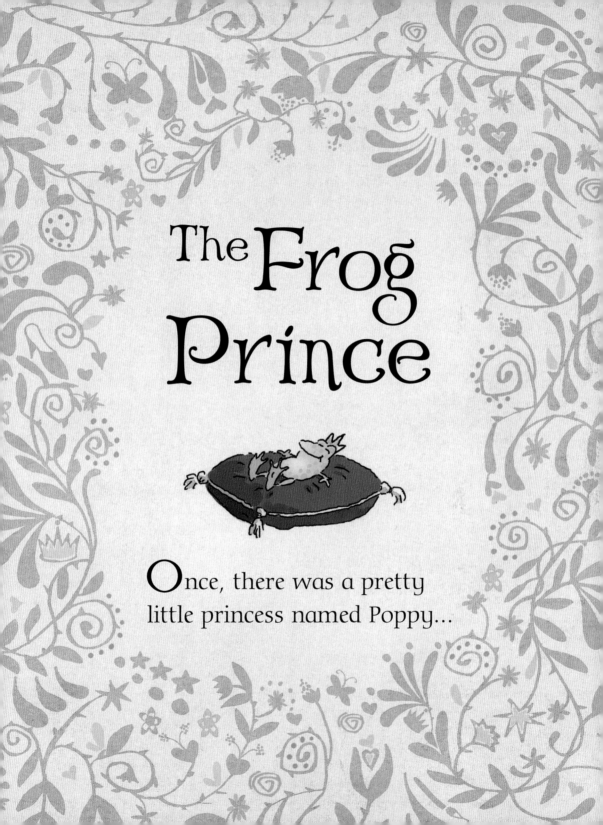

The Frog Prince

Once, there was a pretty
little princess named Poppy...

...and she was furious. "I won't marry Prince Humperdink, Daddy," she said. "He's smelly, smug and slimier than a frog. And he has such big teeth."

"You don't have to marry him until
you're grown up," said her mother.

"I never want to marry him," said Poppy.
"I'd rather eat my toenails."

"That's enough!" said the King. "Stop
your wailing! Prince Humperdink is coming
to dinner tonight and you must be polite to
him. He's a very nice boy, and he is your
future husband, after all."

"I'll find another prince to marry!"
Poppy declared.

"You can have until tomorrow
morning," said the King. "But you'll
never find a prince in that time."

"Just you wait," said Poppy. She picked up
her golden ball and stomped into the garden.

The Frog Prince

Princess Poppy ran down the path to the palace pond, throwing and catching her ball as she went.

"There must be another prince somewhere," she thought.

She was so cross, she didn't see the wobbly stone.

She wibbled...

and wobbled...

and fell face-first...

SPLAT!

...into the pond.

Her beautiful golden ball flew out of her hands. With a loud splash, it disappeared into the deep, dark water.

"Oh no!" Poppy groaned. She looked into the pond, hoping to see her ball.

Instead, she came face to face with a pair of big, bulging eyes.

"Urgh!" Poppy cried. "A frog."

The frog cleared his throat. "Princess Poppy," he croaked. "Let me help you."

Poppy stared in
surprise. "I've never met
a talking frog before,"
she said. "Still, I don't see
how you can help me."

"I can fetch your ball
for you," said the frog.

"Oh," said Poppy. "Thank you."

"But you must promise me
something first," he added.

"Anything!" agreed Poppy.

"Promise you'll let me live in your palace. I want to eat from your plate, drink from your glass and sleep on your silken pillow."

"In your dreams," thought Poppy. But out loud she said, "I promise."

The frog plunged into the pond.

Poppy waited. Suddenly, deep under the water, she saw a glimmer of gold. The frog rose out of the pond, holding the golden ball.

Hooray!

Poppy snatched it up and raced back to the palace.

"Hey!" the frog called after her. "What about your promise?" But Poppy didn't reply.

Wait for me!

The frog hopped as fast as he could after Poppy. When he finally hopped up to the palace door, Poppy slammed it in his face.

Princess Poppy arrived at the palace just in time for supper. She had to sit next to Prince Humperdink, who smelled of cabbage.

Suddenly, they heard a tap at the door.
"Who was that?" said the King.
"No one," Poppy said quickly.

"That's funny," said Prince Humperdink.
"I was sure I heard someone knocking."

The tapping came again.
"Poppy, I really do think someone's there,"
said the King. "I'll ask the footman to look."

"No, Daddy don't!" cried Poppy. "It's only a frog. He rescued my golden ball from the pond, and... I... sort of said he could stay with us."

"Then you must keep your word," bellowed the King. "Let him in."

"But he's wet and warty," said Poppy.

"Poppy!" said her father furiously. "Let that frog in right now!"

As soon as Poppy opened the door, the frog shot inside. He followed her back to her chair. Poppy could hear his wet feet going splat, splat, splat, on the floor behind her.

"Oh dear!" said Prince Humperdink. "Suddenly, I'm not very hungry."

"I'm starving," said the frog. "What's the first course?"

"Cold watercress soup," said the King. "Help yourself!"

The frog dived into Poppy's bowl.

Mmm... delicious...

"What's next?" he asked a maid.

"Um, er..." the maid began nervously.

"Come on!" said the King. "You must know what's for supper."

"Well, your highness," the maid went on, "I'm afraid... it's frogs' legs."

The frog gulped. "I think I might skip this course," he said, weakly.

Poppy didn't usually like frogs' legs, but that night she had seconds... and thirds... and fourths.

"Isn't it time for bed, Princess?" said the frog eventually.

"Oh no!" cried Poppy. "You're not coming anywhere near my bedroom."

"But you promised," said the frog.

You can carry me on a cushion!

Poppy looked pleadingly at her father.

"Come on, dear," said the Queen. "Don't make Poppy touch that green, warty, slimy..."

"Princesses don't break promises," interrupted the King, sternly.

Poppy took a deep breath. Then she reached out and picked up the frog by one foot.

"She touched him!" moaned Prince Humperdink, and fainted.

Poppy dropped the frog in the darkest, most distant corner of her room and climbed into bed.

"But Poppy," said the frog, "you promised I could sleep on your pillow."

"I've had enough!" snapped Poppy. "You're the meanest, ugliest, most horrible frog I've ever met."

"What's more," she added, "if you mention my promise one more time, I'll throw you out of the window."

"No, you won't," said the frog. "You wouldn't dare."

"I do dare," said Poppy. In a fury, she strode over to the frog, picked him up and threw him out of her window.

There was a long silence,
followed by a loud splat.
Poppy suddenly realized what
she'd done. She was horrified.

Frog? Please say something!

"I hope I haven't killed him," she thought.
She raced down the stairs as fast as her legs
could carry her.

Outside, the frog lay sprawled on the palace lawn. Poppy picked him up as gently as she could.

"Are you all right?" she whispered.

"Yes," croaked the frog, carefully feeling his head.

"I didn't mean to hurt you," said Poppy. "I'm so sorry." And she bent down and kissed him.

There was a crash of thunder and a shower of sparks. The frog vanished. In his place stood a handsome young prince.

"At last!" shouted the Prince. "I'm human again. No more slimy skin, no more webbed feet, no more flies..."

One by one, the palace windows flew open and everyone looked out.

"What's going on?" yelled the King. "I'm coming down."

"What happened to you?" Poppy asked the Prince.

"A wicked witch cast a spell on me," he said. "I could only become human again if a princess kissed me."

"So I saved you?" said Poppy proudly.

"Well, yes," said the Prince, "but you did throw me out of the window first."

"Still," said Poppy, "not many princesses would kiss a frog."

"That's true. How can I thank you?" said the Prince.

"Well, you could marry me," replied Poppy.

"Excuse me," said Prince Humperdink, "but Poppy is going to marry ME."

"No I'm not," said Poppy. "It hasn't been arranged yet. And Daddy, you did say I could find my own prince."

"That's true," said the King.

"In that case," said the Prince, getting down on one knee. "If you promise not to throw me out of the window again..."

"I promise," said Poppy.

"Princess Poppy, will you marry me?"

"I will," said Poppy. And she did.

The Elves
and the
Shoemaker

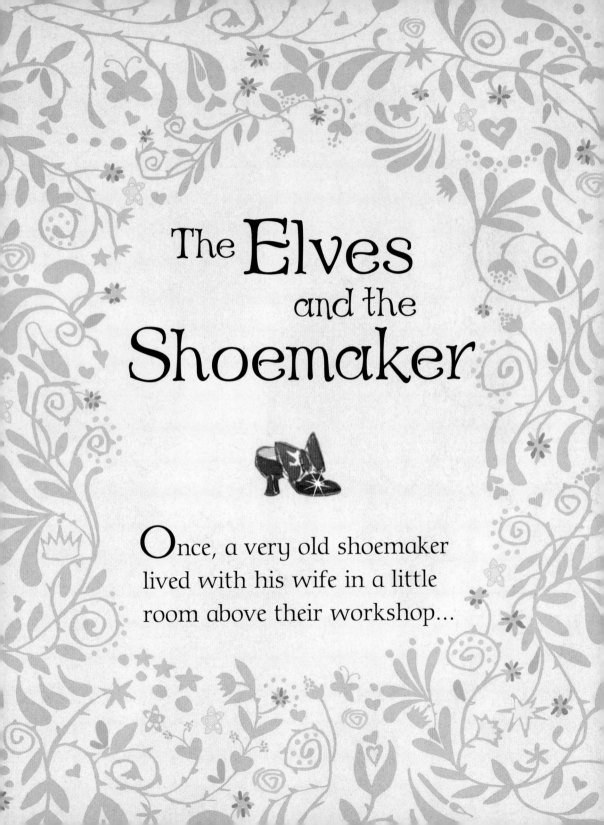

Once, a very old shoemaker
lived with his wife in a little
room above their workshop...

Each day, the
shoemaker drew
different shoe shapes
on his leather.

Then, he carefully
cut out the shapes
with a knife...

and sewed them
together with good,
strong thread.

Next, he stretched the shoe shapes over a wooden foot...

cut out thick soles and made holes in them with a huge needle...

and finally, sewed the soles firmly onto the shoes.

People loved watching the shoemaker at work. Nobody passed his workshop without peeking in.

What splendid shoes!

At the end of the day, there was always a crowd of people waiting to buy his latest shoes.

But, as the years passed, the crowd outside
the workshop grew smaller and smaller.
Some days, no customers came at all.

With very little business, the shoemaker was running out of money. Soon, he could only afford enough leather to make one more pair of shoes.

He cut out the shoe shapes and laid them on his work table. Then he yawned. "I'm too tired to sew these today," he sighed.

Early the next morning, he went downstairs – and stopped in amazement. "Am I dreaming?" he asked himself.

There, on his table, stood a perfect pair of shoes. Someone had neatly sewn up the leather. What's more, they had sewn shiny golden buckles on the front.

The shoemaker was baffled.

He placed the shoes in his window. Before long, a gentleman came in.

"These shoes are divine!" he cried. "They sparkle and shine, and they fit like a glove." And he paid for the shoes with a gold coin.

Now, the shoemaker could afford to make two pairs of shoes. As he cut them out, he yawned. "I'll finish them tomorrow," he thought.

But, by morning, two neat pairs of shoes were waiting for him, fancy bows and all.

That day, the puzzled shoemaker had two more happy customers.

Now, he had enough money to buy leather for four pairs of shoes. After cutting out the leather, the shoemaker went to bed.

The next morning, he couldn't believe his luck. On the table stood four perfect pairs of shoes. "It must be magic!" he cried.

And so it went on. The more leather the shoemaker cut, the more shoes he found in the morning.

Within weeks, business was booming. The shoemaker was a happy man. He had lots of money and little to do. But he still didn't know where the shoes were coming from.

"Who do you think is making our shoes?" whispered the shoemaker.

"I don't know," said his wife, "but let's find out."

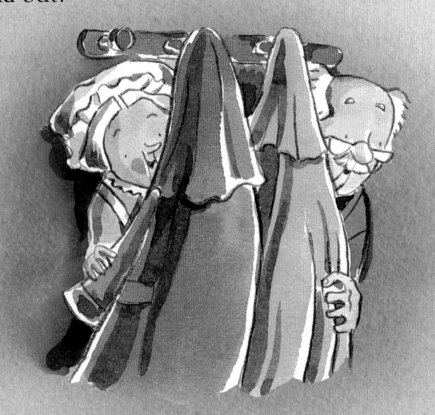

That night, instead of going to bed, they hid behind some coats hanging in a corner of the workshop.

Everything was quiet... until midnight, when two little elves rushed in, wearing nothing but rags. They sat down at the table and quickly began to sew.

They sewed so fast, the shoemaker could hardly see their tiny, nimble fingers.

"What fantastic red boots, even if I do say so myself," said one, admiring his own handiwork.

"They're fit for a queen... or a very tall elf," said the other.

"Hurry up – or we'll be spotted," said the first elf.

"I'm almost done," the second replied. Then they polished the boots until they shone, and left them on the workshop table.

They disappeared through the door, and raced up the street.

The shoemaker and his wife looked at each other, astonished.

"I think I'm going crazy," whispered the shoemaker. "Were those really elves?"

His wife nodded. "How can we ever repay their kindness?" she wondered. "Perhaps I could give them one of my best cabbage and custard crumbles."

"Or... we could make them some new clothes?" said the shoemaker.

"What a splendid idea," she replied, and they set to work.

The shoemaker made two pairs of tiny boots, and his wife spent all day sewing little suits.

That night, instead of leaving leather on the table, the shoemaker left two piles of clothes.

Then he and his wife hid behind the coats again, and waited for the elves.

The elves were delighted with their new outfits. They scrambled into them and danced and skipped all around the room.

I've never worn shoes before!

Wow - my very own shirt!

"How handsome we look!" they cried.
"We're far too grand to work now!"

"Come on," said the first elf. "Let's show
our friends how fine we look!"

The elves skipped merrily out of the
door. The shoemaker and his wife happily
watched them dance up the street.

The shoemaker might have lost his magic helpers, but now he had plenty of customers and wonderful ideas for shoes.

And as for the elves, they never sewed another shoe.

Little Red Riding Hood

Once upon a time there
was a kind little girl...

...who loved to wear a bright red cloak
with a bright red hood.

She wore the cloak so much, she became known as Little Red Riding Hood.

Little Red Riding Hood lived with her mother on the edge of some deep, dark woods.

Map of The Deep Dark Woods
(by Little Red Riding Hood)

Me

Mother Red Riding Hood

Our little cottage

One day, Little Red Riding Hood's mother gave her a pot of vegetable soup.

Granny's cottage

Granny Red Riding Hood

"Take this to your grandmother," she said. "She's not feeling well."

"Now don't you go wandering off," said her mother. "Always remember the rules of the woods."

Rules of the Woods
1. Keep to the path.
2. Don't talk to wolves.

"I will," promised Little Red Riding Hood and she set out along the path. At first, the sun shone brightly and the birds sang.

WANTED
BIG BAD
WOLF!

Little Red Riding Hood skipped happily through the woods.

She hummed a tune to herself...

bent down to tie her shoelace...

...and waved to a woodcutter.

"Good morning," she called.

"Good morning, Little Red Riding Hood," he replied.

Little Red Riding Hood walked deeper
and deeper into the woods...

It grew darker
and darker.

So Little Red Riding Hood didn't see the wolf waiting for her on the path.

And the wolf didn't see Little Red Riding Hood either.

Little Red Riding Hood stepped on the wolf's paw...

and dropped her basket on his head.

"Look where you're going!" said the wolf, huffily.

"But you were right in the middle of the path," said Little Red Riding Hood.

She had forgotten the rule —
don't talk to wolves.

"What have you got in that basket?"
asked the wolf, hungrily.

"Vegetable soup," she replied. "I'm taking
it to my grandmother."

"Vegetables?" cried the wolf. "How revolting! I never touch vegetables. Wolves only eat juicy, red meat."

The wolf was about to gobble up Little Red Riding Hood. But then he had a better idea.

"Perhaps I can eat Little Red Riding Hood *and* her grandmother!" he thought, grinning to himself. "How delicious!"

The wolf put on his softest voice. "Where does your grandmother live?" he asked.

"In the cottage on the other side of the woods," she replied.

"Why don't you take her some flowers?" said the wolf.

Now Little Red Riding Hood forgot the rules again. She wandered off the path to look for flowers...

while the wolf raced off to the grandmother's house.

He knocked lightly on the door.
"Who's there?" asked the grandmother.

"Your granddaughter," squeaked the wolf.
"I've brought you some lovely vegetable soup."

"Let yourself in," said the grandmother. "I'm too weak to get up."

The wolf leaped into the house with a huge roar. He sprang across the room...

...and gobbled up Little Red Riding Hood's grandmother.

Then he climbed into bed to wait for Little Red Riding Hood. Soon, there was a knock at the door. "Come on in," he called.

Little Red Riding Hood looked at her grandmother. "Oh Grandmother," she said, "What big ears you have."

"All the better to hear you with," said the wolf.

Little Red Riding Hood came closer to the bed. "Oh Grandmother," she said. "What big eyes you have."

"All the better to see you with," said the wolf.

"Oh Grandmother," she said. "What big hairy hands you have."

"All the better to hug you with," said the wolf.

"But Grandmother," she cried, "what big sharp teeth you have."

"All the better to eat you with," snapped the wolf. And he jumped out of bed and gobbled her up.

The wolf licked his lips and fell fast asleep, snoring. He snored so loudly that the woodcutter heard him.

"I've never heard the old woman snore *that* loudly," he thought. "I'll just make sure she's okay."

"Oh no," thought the woodcutter, as he strode into the cottage. "The wolf's eaten the old woman..."

"But perhaps I can still save her!"
He picked up some scissors and snipped open the wolf's tummy.

Snip, snip... He saw a bright red hood.
Snip, snip... Little Red Riding Hood's head
popped out.

Snippety-snip, faster and faster...
The woodcutter kept cutting until
Grandmother popped out too.

Quick as a flash, Little Red Riding Hood ran outside and picked up lots of stones. She put them in the wolf's tummy and sewed it up.

Rattle
rattle
rattle

Then the wolf woke up. He tried to sneak out of the door, but the stones rattled inside him.

"Now everyone can hear me coming – I'll never catch anyone," cried the wolf.

"Exactly!" said the woodcutter.

"You'll just have to eat vegetables instead," laughed Little Red Riding Hood.

From that day,
the wolf lived on
boiled carrots.
He never ate
another person.

As for Little Red Riding Hood, she never,
ever talked to a wolf again.

Cinderella

There once was a young girl,
whose name was Cinderella...

...her mother had died when she was very young. Her father married again, and his new wife was spiteful and snooty.

Her daughters were even worse – they treated Cinderella like a servant.

"What's little Cinders doing today then?" teased Griselda.

"She's sweeping away cobwebs, like a servant," sneered Grimella.

"Get on with it then, servant girl," said Griselda.

Just then, Cinderella's stepmother appeared, holding a letter.

"Griselda, Grimella," she cried. "I have the most exciting news. The Prince is giving a Christmas Ball and you're invited."

"May I go to the Ball as well?" Cinderella asked hopefully.

"You must be joking," her stepmother replied. "You belong in the kitchen."

Cinderella turned to her father, but he coughed and looked away. "He's too scared of Stepmother to help me," thought Cinderella.

"We'll be the most beautiful girls there," chorused the stepsisters.

"I'm sure the Prince will want to marry one of you," said their mother, proudly beaming.

All that week, boot-makers, dressmakers, jewellers, wig-makers and hairdressers streamed through the door.

Cinderella tried to make her
stepsisters look as pretty as possible.
It wasn't easy.

At first, Grimella wanted to wear a hat
decorated with stuffed birds. Griselda chose
a lime green dress with bright yellow spots.

Cinderella worked night and day, putting the finishing touches to their outfits. At last they were ready.

Cinderella's stepsisters gazed at themselves in the mirror. "Don't we look gorgeous!" they shrieked.

"Oh my Tinkerbells, you look wonderful," gasped their mother. "The coach is here. Let's go!"

The front door was opened. There was a swish of skirts and a blast of cold air. Then Cinderella was left alone.

A loud crash in the chimney made Cinderella look up. There, in the fireplace, covered in soot from head to toe, was her godmother.

"Godmother Felicity," cried Cinderella, "whatever are you doing in our chimney?"

"I missed the door," Felicity replied airily, as she bustled into the room.

"But I haven't seen you since I was ten," said Cinderella.

"I've been with Sleeping Beauty, my other godchild," said Felicity. "But she wouldn't wake up, so it was rather dull."

Felicity peered at Cinderella. "Have you been crying?" she asked.

"Yes! I wanted to go to the Ball, but I'm not allowed."

"Well, you can wipe those tears away, girlie. Fantastic Felicity is here to help. Now, go and fetch me a large pumpkin."

"Great," thought Cinderella, "my stepsisters are at the Ball and I'm picking pumpkins for my crazy godmother."

"Here you are," Cinderella said, a few minutes later. "It's the biggest one."

"Jolly good," Felicity replied. "The time has come to tell you a great secret...

Your godmother is a fairy. Watch this!" Felicity flicked her wand and cried, "Abracadabra, cadabra cadeen!"

There was a tinkle of music and a shower
of sparks. In the place of the pumpkin stood
a beautiful golden coach. Cinderella gasped.
"You really can do magic!"

"This is just the beginning," Felicity replied.
"Now, where can I find your mousetrap?"

"Under the sink," said Cinderella. Felicity peered in. "Six mice, one fat rat, all alive. Excellent. Open the trap."

As the mice came out, Felicity tapped each one with her wand.

One by one, the mice were transformed into fine white horses. The rat became a rosy-cheeked coachman, with very large whiskers.

"Now I need six lizards," said Felicity. "Hmm... I expect there'll be some behind your watering can."

"There are!" said Cinderella, handing them to her godmother. In a flash, the lizards became footmen.

They were dressed in glistening green and looked as if they'd been footmen all their lives.

Finally, Felicity touched Cinderella with her wand. A moment later, her rags turned into a dazzling dress of gold and silver.

On her feet was a perfect pair of dainty glass slippers.

"There's just one problem," said Felicity. "You must leave before twelve. On the last stroke of midnight, my magic will fade."

"I promise," Cinderella replied, climbing into the coach. "Thank you so much," she called, as the horses swept her away.

When Cinderella entered the ballroom, everyone fell silent. Then a whisper went around the room.

"Who's that beautiful girl?" the ladies wondered.

A voice next to Cinderella almost made her jump. It was the Prince.

"May I have this dance?" he asked.

Cinderella and the Prince twirled across the floor.

"She's so graceful," said the other ladies. "And look at her dress! Have you ever seen anything so delicate?"

"The Prince is only being polite," snapped Grimella. "He'd much rather dance with me."

As the Prince whirled Cinderella around the room, she caught sight of the clock. It was almost midnight.

"Oh no!" she said. "I must go." And she ran away across the dance floor.

The Prince raced after her. "Come back," he called. But Cinderella had disappeared into the darkness.

The Prince turned back to the palace with a sigh. Then something on the steps caught his eye. "Her glass slipper!" he cried.

Cinderella ran home as
fast as she could. She arrived
just before her stepsisters.

The next morning, the entire street was woken by the shout of a town crier, who was followed by a messenger.

Hear ye, hear ye!

By the order of his royal highness, the Prince, every girl in the kingdom must try on this glass slipper. The Prince will marry its true owner.

Cinderella's stepmother flung open the door and grabbed the messenger. "One of my girls will fit this shoe," she said proudly, "and then we'll be royalty."

Griselda couldn't even fit her big toe in the shoe. She pushed until her foot was bright red.

"Give it here!" shouted Grimella, ramming half her foot in the shoe. It got stuck.

"You useless child," cried her mother. She wrenched the slipper off Grimella's foot and flung it at the messenger. "Off you go then," she snapped.

"Excuse me, ma'am," the messenger said, "I've strict orders that *every* young lady is to try on the shoe." He looked at Cinderella.

"She's just a servant," said Grimella.

Cinderella's father coughed. "Actually, Cinderella has every right to try on the slipper," he said bravely.

She walked over to the messenger and slipped on the shoe. It was a perfect fit.

"No!" shrieked Griselda and Grimella.
"She can't be a princess," shouted their
mother. "I won't allow it."

With one swift movement, the messenger swept off his hat and cloak. Everyone in the room gasped. It was the Prince.

He knelt in front of Cinderella. "I've been searching everywhere for you," he said. "Will you marry me?"

"Oh yes!" she replied.
At that moment,
there was a puff of
smoke and Felicity flew
into the room.

"Time for a little
more magic,"
she declared.

Felicity flicked her wand and gave Cinderella a dress even more beautiful than the one she had worn to the Ball.

"My princess!" said the Prince, and swept Cinderella off to his palace. They were married the very next day... and lived happily ever after.

But Griselda and Grimella
were not so happy.

Their mother never stopped
scolding them. "It's all your fault for
having such big feet," she told them.

The Swan Princess

Far away and long ago, there
lived a little girl named Eliza...

...who was the King's only daughter. The Queen had died when Eliza was born, but she had a kind father and eleven older brothers to look after her.

When her brothers went to school, Eliza looked at beautiful picture books, or watched swallows swoop past. She couldn't have been happier.

The Swan Princess

Then, one bitterly cold winter, the King married again. His new wife was tall and elegant, and everyone admired her. But she had a dark secret. The new Queen was a witch!

The Queen hated
the King's children, and she
vowed to get rid of them.
She spent her days alone
inside the palace, stroking
her warty pet toads, and
dreaming up spiteful spells.

A week later, the princes came home from school to find the Queen barring their way.

"You're not wanted here," she shouted. "Fly away like wild birds!"

The horrified princes
began to sprout white feathers.
One by one, they turned into
swans and flew out to sea.

The Queen went inside and told the
King the princes had run away.

Now there was just Eliza...

The Queen didn't dare cast another spell in case the King grew suspicious.

But, as the years passed, Eliza grew so beautiful that the Queen could bear her jealousy no longer.

One night, she secretly dropped her toads into Eliza's bath and whispered some magic words.

These three toads will make Eliza **ugly**, **stupid** and **wicked**!

Eliza was too good to
be enchanted by such
an evil spell. When she
stepped into the bath, the
toads turned into flowers.
Their red petals floated
gently on the water.

The Queen was
furious. She needed
a new plan.

When Eliza finished her bath, the Queen made her sit down, away from the mirror. Then she wiped Eliza's face with walnut juice, and tangled her hair while pretending to comb it.

Now Eliza looked nothing like her beautiful self. Her father didn't even recognize her.

"Who let this wild creature in?" he shouted. "Take it away!"

The guards tried to seize her.

Eliza slipped between them and ran out of the castle, sobbing. She fled to the forest to hide.

Eliza wandered through the forest
until she came to a lake. She knelt down
and washed her face with the cool,
refreshing water.

As the sun set, Eliza looked around to
see where she might spend the night.

Something in the distance caught her eye.
A group of swans was flying over the trees.

They shook their wings and, to
Eliza's astonishment, instead of swans,
her brothers stood before her.

Eliza was overjoyed. When they had all
finished hugging, Prince Julian told her
what had happened.

"The Queen's spell
turned us into swans,"
he explained, "but we become human again
at night. Tomorrow, we must fly back to
our new home."

"I'm coming with you," Eliza decided.

Eliza and her brothers spent all night weaving a net of rushes, so the swans would be able to carry her.

As the sun rose, the swans lifted Eliza into the air and they flew far over the sea.

As dusk fell, they landed. Once again, the swans shed their feathers.

"This is our home now," Julian told Eliza, showing her a cave carpeted with soft, green moss.

That night, Eliza dreamed she was still flying through the clouds.

In the dream, a beautiful fairy appeared before her.

"Eliza," she said. "You can save your brothers from the Queen's spell. You must make each one a shirt of nettles. When they put on the shirts, the spell will be broken."

"But you must make the shirts in silence," the fairy warned. "If you speak a word before the spell is ended, your brothers will die."

Eliza reached out to touch a nettle. It stung her fingers – and she woke up.

The next day, Eliza set to work. She picked huge armfuls of nettles, and started to weave them together. They stung her hands, but she didn't make a sound.

By evening, her fingers were covered in blisters, but Eliza didn't mind. She had almost finished the first shirt.

When the princes saw her weaving, they
knew what Eliza was trying to do. They
thanked her, but she could not reply.

Prince Jasper wept to see her fingers. Where
his tears touched her skin, it healed at once.

The next day, Eliza set off to pick
some more nettles, and stopped in
an overgrown churchyard.
"What is your name?" called
a voice from behind her.

Eliza spun around, to see a handsome king
watching her.
"What are you doing in my grounds?" the
King asked her. "And why are you picking
nettles?" But Eliza could not reply.

"She can't talk," the King realized. "Come back to my palace," he said gently, "and I'll look after you."

Eliza shook her head, but it was no good. The King led her through his gardens and into his vast palace.

Before long, the King was in love with the strange, silent girl. When she spent all day weaving nettles, he gave her soft gloves to cover her blistered fingers. And his kindness made Eliza love him in return.

Soon the King had made up his mind. "Will you marry me?" he asked Eliza. She smiled and nodded.

The King summoned his Archbishop. "I'm getting married," he told him.

The Archbishop threw up his hands in horror. He thought Eliza was a witch. "You hardly know the girl!" he cried.

"I don't care," said the King. "I'll marry her anyway."

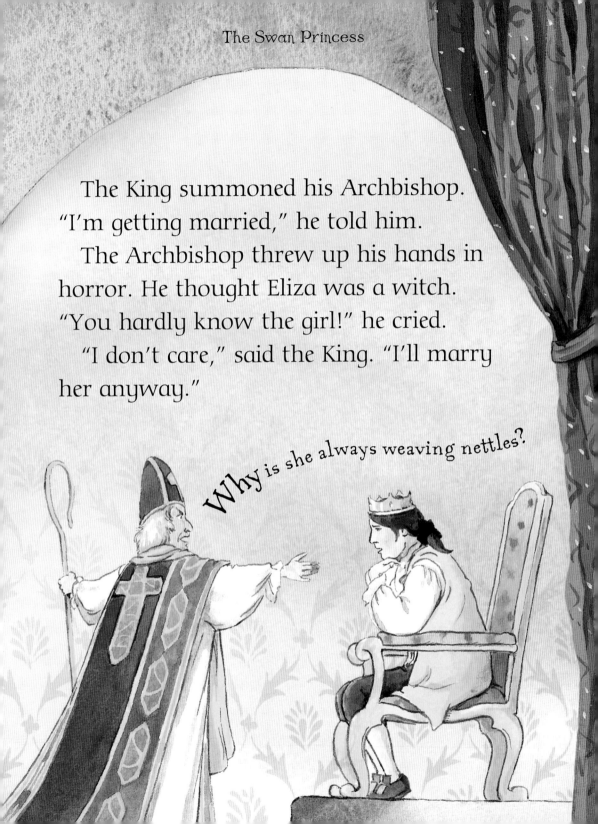

Why is she always weaving nettles?

Meanwhile, Eliza wove busily. By the night before the wedding, she had made ten shirts. "I'll finish the last one tonight," she thought happily.

As she started the final shirt, she realized she needed more nettles. "I'll just have to go and pick some," she decided.

Outside, it was so dark she could barely see the graveyard. She shivered. "There's no such thing as ghouls or ghosts!" she told herself bravely.

The Archbishop was still awake, worrying about the wedding.

He saw Eliza slip out and decided to follow her. "Only a witch would pick nettles at midnight," he told himself.

When Eliza began wandering among the tombstones, he decided he had seen enough.

"Stop, witch!" he cried.
His shout brought the
palace guards running. On
his orders, they seized Eliza
and threw her into prison.

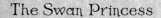

The next day, instead of a wedding, there was a trial. Eliza was brought before the judge in chains.

"I saw her picking nettles in the graveyard at midnight," the Archbishop cried. "She must be a witch!"

"Well, what do you say to that?" the judge asked Eliza. But she could not speak to defend herself.

The judge frowned. "The girl is a witch. She will be executed tomorrow."

The King was heartbroken, but there was nothing he could do.

Eliza was thrown into a tiny prison cell and her shirts were thrown in after her. "I'd nearly finished them," she thought desperately, "but now I'll never see my brothers again!" She felt completely miserable.

Suddenly, something fluttered against the window. Eliza looked up – and saw Jasper looking back at her.

She held up the shirts so Jasper could see them. He bowed his head and then flew away.

"I mustn't give up," Eliza told herself. She spent all night weaving the final shirt. At dawn, there was just one sleeve left to make. And then she ran out of nettles.

Minutes later, there was a bang on the door. The guards had come to take her away. They led her outside, still clutching the shirts.

A huge crowd had gathered to see the execution. Before it could start, there was a startled murmur and people began pointing at the sky. Eleven white swans were flying closer and closer.

The swans swooped down. One by one, they swept past Eliza, so she could throw the shirts over them. The crowd gasped.

There was a shimmering in the air and then, instead of the swans, eleven young men stood beside Eliza.

At the same time, Eliza's chains turned into white roses and fell to the ground. The spell was finally broken – and Eliza could speak.

"Oh Jasper," cried Eliza, "you've still got a swan's wing!"

"I don't mind," he replied, giving her a big, feathery hug.

Then the King spoke. "I don't know what's going on here," he said, "but perhaps you can tell me at the wedding feast..."

"…if you still want to marry me?" he continued, turning shyly to Eliza.

"Oh yes!" said Eliza, smiling. "And there won't be any witches at this wedding – I promise."

The Emperor's New Clothes

Once upon a time, there was an
emperor who adored clothes...

...in fact, he was so crazy about clothes, he didn't care about anything else. He ignored his soldiers and avoided his advisors.

He preferred to spend all day in front of his mirror, trying on gorgeous gowns and preposterous pantaloons…

...and he only liked riding in the park so he could show off each fabulous new outfit.

I know.

But the Emperor had a problem. The royal procession was in two weeks' time, and he had nothing to wear.

"You must have something, Your Excellence," said Boris, his servant. "You already have seven thousand, three hundred and thirty-two outfits."

"But I've worn them all before," moaned the Emperor.

"I want to look so splendiferous that people will talk about me for years to come. Go and find me the finest clothes-makers in town," he ordered.

"I'm off to have a snooze," the Emperor added. "It's been a rather tiring morning."

Boris spent all day looking for an incredible outfit. He wasn't having much luck, until...

FLOUR

URGENT!
Emperor needs
tasteful
and elegant
new outfit!
Clothes-makers
apply here.

...two strangers rushed up to him.

"We're the finest clothes-makers in the world," they said. "Take us to the Emperor at once."

When they arrived at the palace, the strangers burst straight into the Emperor's private bedroom.

"Who are you?" shouted
the Emperor, angrily.
"We are Slimus..."

"and Slick..."

"at your service,"
they said.

The Emperor just stared at them.

"Haven't you heard of us?" said Slimus, looking shocked.

"Um, well... no," admitted the Emperor. He hated not knowing things.

"We make magical clothes!" said Slimus.
"Magical?" said the Emperor.

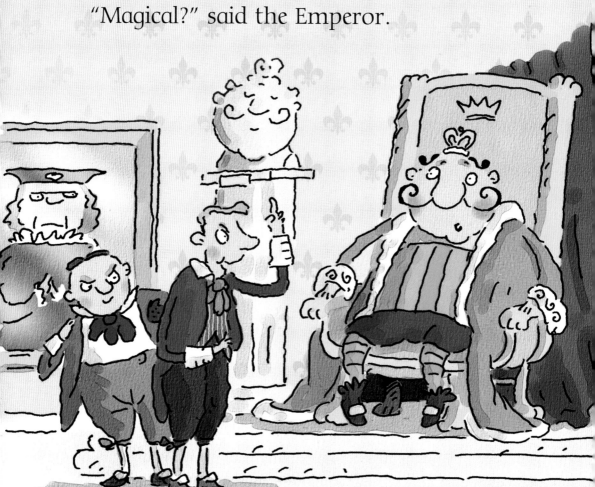

"Yes," said Slick. "Our clothes can only be seen by clever people. They will be invisible to anyone stupid."

"Anyone who can't do their job properly won't be able to see them either," Slimus added, with a sly smile.

Boris gulped. "What if I can't see the clothes?" he thought.

The Emperor was very excited. "Make me a magic suit this minute," he cried.

"It won't be cheap," replied Slimus and Slick.

"Take this," said the Emperor, handing them a sack of money. "You can work in the palace – take anything you want. Is there anything else I can get you?"

"We will also need five fudge cakes, ten tubs of vanilla ice cream and a constant supply of your finest chocolate," said Slimus.

"That would really help our work," added Slick.

As soon as they were alone, Slimus and Slick laughed until their bellies ached and their faces turned purple.

"The fool believed us!" cried Slimus. "We're going to have lots and lots of lovely money."

Slimus and Slick set up their workshop in the palace. They told the Emperor that he couldn't see the suit until it was finished.

Every day the Emperor crept past their door. Finally, Slimus and Slick invited him to see the splendid new outfit.

"Oh Your Excellence," said Slimus, bowing low. "We're so delighted to see you!"
The Emperor looked at the loom.

He looked again. "This is terrible," he thought. "I can't see anything at all. I'm not worthy of being Emperor!"

But aloud he said, "It's magnificent."
"Oh crumbs," thought Boris, "I can't see
a thing." He gulped. "How tasteful," he said.

The palace footmen were worried. Each
thought the other could see the magical
material. "Splendid," they said in unison.

Slimus and Slick pretended to take the material down from the loom. They made cuts in the air with huge scissors and sewed using needles without any thread.

Everyone clapped loudly. The Emperor even gave Slimus and Slick medals for their excellent sewing.

On the morning of the royal procession, the Emperor went to put on his new clothes. He was filled with nervous excitement.

"Would Your Majesty care to undress?" said Slimus. "I'll bring over the cloak and the train."

"This is your shirt, Your Majesty," said Slick. "See, it's as light as a spider's web."

Then the palace footmen bent down, as if they were picking up a train. The Emperor admired himself in the mirror one last time.

"Don't I look splendid, Boris?" the Emperor asked.

"Yes, Your Excellence," said Boris, looking straight up at the ceiling.

"Then," said the Emperor, "let the royal procession begin."

The crowd gasped
as the Emperor emerged
from the palace. Everyone
had heard that only clever
people could see his clothes.

"What a splendid outfit," they cried.
"Such a magnificent pattern," they said
to each other.

The Emperor smiled to himself. "These are my most successful clothes ever," he thought, and added a spring to his step.

"Let me see him," cried a small child, who was stuck at the back of the crowd.

The child was lifted up on his father's shoulders, so he could see the Emperor in all his glory.

"Ooh!" said the child. "The Emperor's got nothing on!"

Everyone around the child fell silent and looked at the Emperor again.

"He's right you know," said his father.
"The Emperor is naked!"
Then, faster than a spreading fire, a
whisper whizzed through the crowd.

The Emperor's got no clothes on!

Soon, the whole crowd was chanting.

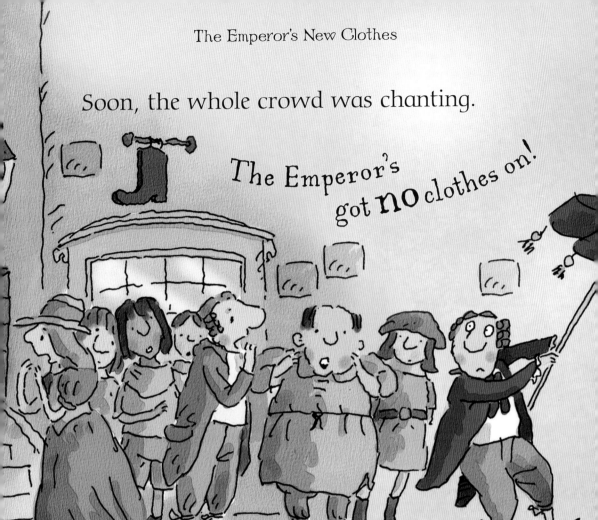

The Emperor's got **no** clothes on!

The Emperor heard their words and
shivered. Suddenly, he felt very cold.

The Emperor looked down. To his horror,
he saw that they were right. Then he
blushed bright red – all over.

"I must carry on," he thought. "This is the royal procession – and I am the Emperor." He held his head high and walked more proudly than ever.

Meanwhile, Slimus and Slick were packing their bags full of money, getting ready to flee the palace forever.

A toast to *invisible* clothes... and *naked* emperors!

"We tricked him!" they cried, and cackled with glee.

As for the crowds – they were enjoying the best procession ever. Boris, of course, wasn't having such a good day...

"Oh well," he thought, as he followed the Emperor home. "At least one thing turned out the way he wanted. People will talk about the Emperor's new clothes for years to come."

Hans Christian Andersen

Hans Christian Andersen was born in Odense, a little town in Denmark, in 1805. His father was a shoemaker and his mother was a washerwoman, and they were very poor. Hans left home to seek his fortune when he was still a young boy, and became a writer. He was inspired by the stories he heard in Odense as a child, where the old women still told traditional tales – and half-believed them, too. He wrote fairy tales based on these stories, and became famous all over the world.

The Brothers Grimm

Jacob and Wilhelm Grimm were brothers who lived in Germany in the early 1800s. They journeyed from village to village in the German countryside, collecting fairy tales. The Grimms published hundreds of these during their lifetime, gathering them into large volumes of tales.

Cinderella

One of the earliest versions of Cinderella, "Rhodopis and the Rose-red Slippers", was written down in Ancient Egypt more than 2,000 years ago. There have been over 700 versions since. Cinderella has been known as Rashin Coatie in Scotland, Zezolla in Italy and the Flowerpot Princess in Japan. The version in this book is based on a retelling by Charles Perrault, a French writer who lived in the 17th century.

Beauty and the Beast

Beauty and the Beast was first written down in 1740 by a French woman called Gabrielle de Villeneuve. It was retold a few years later by another French writer, Marie Le Prince de Beaumont, and there have been many retellings since. The version in this book is based on both Villeneuve's and Beaumont's stories.

Additional design by Brenda Cole
Digital manipulation by John Russell, Mike Wheatley and Nick Wakeford